Eric Maddern

has written many books for Frances Lincoln
including *Earth Story, Curious Clownfish, Rainbow Bird*
and *Spirit of the Forest* (with Helen East and Alan Marks).
The Fire Children, illustrated by Frané Lessac,
was chosen for Junior Education Books of the Year 1993
and selected for Children's Books
of the Year 1994.

Paul Hess's

books include Malachy Doyle's *Hungry! Hungry! Hungry!*
and *The Great Castle of Marshmangle*, Julia Donaldson's
Giants and the Joneses, Josephine Poole's *Jack and the Beanstalk*
and Alan MacDonald's *Pig in a Wig*. His first book for
Frances Lincoln was *Hidden Tales from Eastern Europe*,
by Antonia Barber.

Eric Maddern's and Paul Hess's other books
for Frances Lincoln are *The King with Horse's Ears,*
Death in a Nut and *Nail Soup*.

993156378 8

FOR SALE

To Tomos, Eilir, Mali, Urien and Lleu — E.M.
For Karen — P.H.

How to pronounce the names
Shon (Welsh spelling Sion) is pronounced "Shorn"
Sian is pronounced "Sharn"

GLOUCESTERSHIRE COUNTY LIBRARY	
9931563788	
PETERS	25-Feb-08
	£5.99

The Cow on the Roof copyright © Frances Lincoln Limited 2006
Text copyright © Eric Maddern 2006
Illustrations copyright © Paul Hess 2006

First published in Great Britain and the USA in 2006 by
Frances Lincoln Children's Books, 4 Torriano Mews
Torriano Avenue, London NW5 2RZ
www.franceslincoln.com

Distributed in the USA by Publishers Group West

First paperback edition 2007

All rights reserved
No part of this publication may be reproduced, stored in a retrieval system, or transmitted,
in any form, or by any means, electrical, mechanical, photocopying, recording or otherwise
without the prior written permission of the publisher or a licence permitting restricted copying.
In the United Kingdom such licences are issued by the Copyright Licensing Agency,
Saffron House, 6-10 Kirby Street, London EC1N 8TS.

British Library Cataloguing in Publication Data available on request

ISBN 978-1-84507-591-0

Illustrated with watercolours

Set in Deepdene

Printed in China

1 3 5 7 9 8 6 4 2

The Cow on the Roof

Eric Maddern

Illustrated by Paul Hess

F

FRANCES LINCOLN
CHILDREN'S BOOKS

Once upon a time there was a man called Shon and a woman called Sian. They lived in a little cottage on a hill. The roof of the cottage was covered with grass, green growing grass.

Every day Shon went out to the fields. Sometimes he ploughed the soil. Sometimes he sowed the seeds. Sometimes he weeded the turnips. And sometimes he cut the hay. There was plenty to do and he was always tired when he got home. But Sian, who stayed at home and worked around the farmyard, always seemed as fresh as a buttercup.

After a while, Shon started to feel that he was the one doing all the hard work. And he began to grumble. He began to complain. He began to moan.

At last Sian could bear it no longer, so she said: "All right, Shon, if that's the way you feel, tomorrow I'll go out and do your work, and you can stay at home and do mine."

"*Great!*" said Shon. "Tomorrow I'll have a rest, I'll have a holiday, I'll have a day off!"

The next day, Sian went off with the scythe over her shoulder and Shon stoked the fire, put his feet up and lit his pipe.

"**Ah,** *this is the life,*" he thought, and he sat for two whole hours doing absolutely nothing.

But suddenly Shon realised he had to make butter to go with their dinner-time porridge. He knew how to make it, though he'd never actually done it himself. So he got the churn, poured in the cream and began *turning and churning, turning and churning.*

After a while he looked inside. Just cream sloshing about. So he turned the handle faster still, *turning and churning, turning and churning.* Again he looked inside. Still no butter.

By now Shon was hot and tired. For a third time he turned, faster than ever, **turning and churning, turning and churning.** But once again, still no butter!

Now Shon was really thirsty.

"I know, I'll go to the cellar and pour a drink of ale."

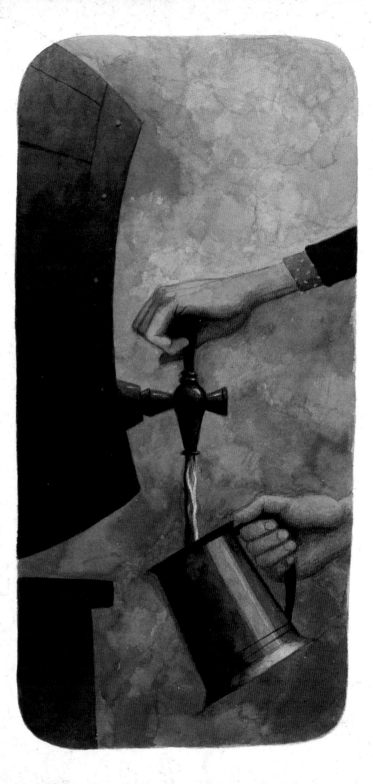

He went down the steps into the cellar. There at the bottom stood a keg of fine, homemade brown ale. He turned the tap and began pouring the ale into a mug. Oh, it looked good. It had a dark colour, a frothy head and a smell that made his mouth water. He could hardly wait.

But suddenly there was a loud bang and a squeal and a clatter from upstairs.

"*Oh no!*" cried Shon, and he dropped the mug and ran quickly back up into the kitchen.

He'd left the kitchen door open, and there was the pig. It had knocked over the churn, spilled cream all over the floor and was greedily lapping it up.

Shon was furious. He booted the pig out of the kitchen, then looked at the mess.

"Oh well," he said, shrugging his shoulders. *"Gone is gone."*

Then Shon remembered. He had left the ale running from the keg downstairs. He raced back down the steps, but it was too late. Every last drop of ale was sloshing about on the cellar floor.

Oh no! This was terrible, far worse than spilling the cream. But there was nothing he could do about it, so he shrugged his shoulders once more and said,

"Oh well. Gone is gone."

Shon went back into the kitchen. There was no more cream, but at least he could still make the porridge.

But first he had to roll the oats. So he took a tray, filled it with oats, found a special rolling pin with grooves in it and began to roll the oats.

Then outside in the barn the cow began to moo.

"Oh dear," said Shon. "I'll have to take the cow to the field."

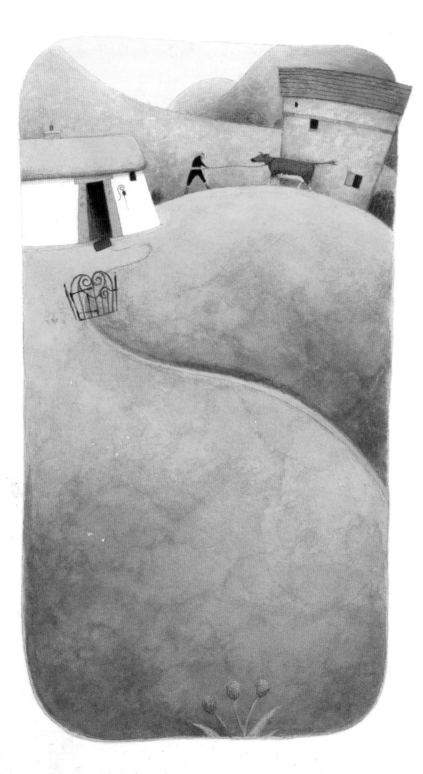

He left the oats, went to the barn and put a rope around the cow's neck. He was just thinking about the porridge and how far it was to the field, when he noticed, growing on the cottage roof, fresh, juicy grass.

"I know," he thought. "I'll put the cow on the roof."

So Shon led the cow to the hill behind the cottage and put a plank to the roof. At first she wouldn't go up, but at last he coaxed her with a handful of sweet grass. Then he took the rope's end and dropped it down the chimney.

"I'll tie that off when I get down, just to be sure she's safe."

Shon left the cow munching away on the roof and went back to the kitchen.

Oh no! He'd left the door open and this time the hens had come in.

They'd found the oats, scratched and scattered them over the floor. And they'd left

chicken droppings mixed in with the cream. Ugh! **What a mess!**

Shon shooed the chickens out and then said to himself, *"Oh well. Gone is gone."*

But he still had some oats so he put them with water into a pot.

He was stoking the fire when he noticed the dangling rope. He grabbed the end and tied it round his ankle, thinking, "Now I'll know what the cow's doing on the roof.".

And then he began to stir the porridge.

The porridge was just starting to thicken when the cow fell off the roof! Shon was yanked by his ankle up the chimney, where he stuck upside-down. Outside the poor cow was hanging by her neck, her feet just touching the ground, crying, *"Mooeeaagh! Mooeeaagh!!!"*

Meanwhile, out in the fields, Sian had been
working hard all day. She looked up at the sun
and realised it was past her dinner-time.
So she began walking back to the cottage.

When she came in sight of the house,
there was the cow hanging off the roof!
So she ran up to it, pulled the axe out of
the chopping-block and chopped the rope.

Inside, Shon fell headfirst down the chimney
and *into the pot of porridge.*

When Sian opened the door, there was Shon with soot up to his armpits and porridge over his head.

What a mess!

Sian looked at the cream and the oats, the chicken and the pig droppings. She sniffed the ale wafting from the cellar. Then she smiled and said:

"Oh well, gone is gone. But from now on, you stick to your work, I'll stick to mine, and we'll say no more about it."

"I'm sorry, my dear, I was wrong," said Shon. "Your work is just as hard as mine."

The next day Shon strode off to the fields and never once complained again.

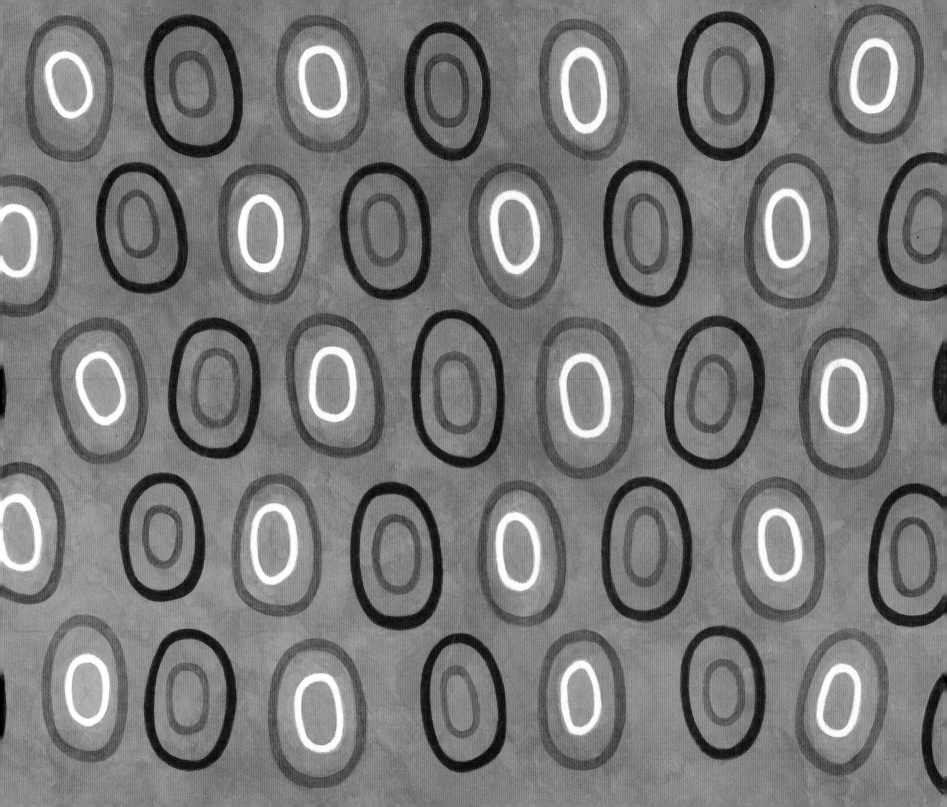

OTHER PICTURE BOOKS FROM FRANCES LINCOLN CHILDREN'S BOOKS

The King with Horse's Ears

Eric Maddern

Illustrated by Paul Hess

No one knows about King Mark's ears except his barber.
Keeping the secret eventually drives him to the doctor, who advises
him to whisper it to the ground. But sooner or later, truth will out...
Delightfully droll artwork by Paul Hess helps demonstrate
that being different can be an advantage!

ISBN 978-0-7112-2079-9 (UK)
ISBN 978-1-84507-309-1 (US)

Death in a Nut

Eric Maddern

Illustrated by Paul Hess

When Jack meets Old Man Death coming up the beach to his cottage,
he knows at once what's up. "You're not taking my mother!" he cries,
and piles into Death with his fists. With each punch, Death gets smaller,
until Jack can squeeze him into a hazelnut shell. He throws the nut
out to sea and goes home – but then the trouble begins...
A thoughtful story of how, without death, there can be no life.

ISBN 978-1-84507-277-3

Frances Lincoln titles are available from all good bookshops.
You can also buy books and find out more about your favourite titles,
authors and illustrators at our website: www.franceslincoln.com.